For Mrs. Pea and our four little peas—K. P.

To my two little peas, Dara and Walter—A. W.

ALADDIN

An imprint of Simon & Schuster Children's Publishing Division
1230 Avenue of the Americas, New York, New York 10020
First Aladdin hardcover edition June 2021
Text copyright © 2019 by Kjartan Poskitt | Illustrations copyright © 2019 by Alex Willmore
Originally published in Great Britain in 2019 by Simon & Schuster UK Ltd
For information about special discounts for bulk purchases, please contact Simon & Schuster Special Sales
at 1-866-506-1949 or business@simonandschuster.com.
The Simon & Schuster Speakers Bureau can bring authors to your live event. For more information
or to book an event contact the Simon & Schuster Speakers Bureau at 1-866-248-3049
or visit our website at www.simonspeakers.com.
The text of this book was set in Archer.
Manufactured in Malaysia 0321 SUK
2 4 6 8 10 9 7 5 3 1
Library of Congress Control Number 2020942719
ISBN 978-1-5344-9014-7 | ISBN 978-1-5344-9015-4 (eBook)

THE RUNAWAY PEA

Kjartan Poskitt & Alex Willmore

ALADDIN

New York London Toronto Sydney New Delhi

Dinner is ready, but what do we see?
Something's escaping ...

A RUNAWAY PEA!

He pinged off the plate with incredible force . . .

... then slipped and went

SPLAT

in a puddle of sauce.

The carrots and beans were all laughing with glee—
"You didn't get far, you piddling pea."

"Just watch!" said the pea.
"I've hardly begun.

I might only be small,
but I want to have fun."

The pea shot away with a skip and a hop . . .

... then into the dog bowl he fell with a

PLOP!

Climb, little pea! Climb up the side—
QUICK, before Boris's mouth opens wide!

The runaway pea jumped amazingly high
and so nearly landed in Boris's eye!

He rolled along Boris's back in a flash,
but a flick of the tail sent him flying off . . .

"Get out of my tank!"
said Adele with a SQUIRT!

He fell on a mousetrap, which snapped with a **BANG...**

and bounced off a cobweb
that stretched and went

TWANG!

He came to a rest on a high, dusty shelf.
"So far, so good!" smiled the pea to himself.

"Surely there's nothing else left to go wrong?"

Then a fan started up and it blew him along.

And what's that below with an orangey glow?
It's the slot in the top of the toaster . . .

OH NO!

In the pea fell, unable to stop,

"OWWWWW."

cried the pea, "my bottom's on fire,"

as he flew straight on into the tumbling dryer.

Buffered

and battered

and bounced all about,

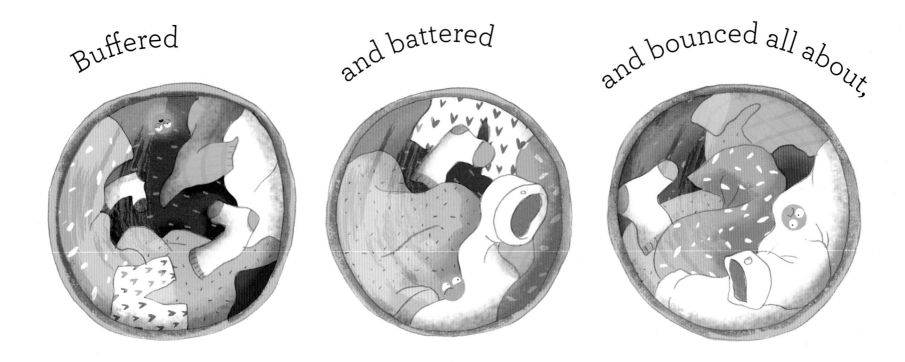

the pea was so glad when he finally got out.

He collapsed on a shirt that
had newly been washed . . .

LOOK OUT, little pea, or you're going to get squashed!

He tumbled and rolled along out of control . . .

. . . under the fridge to
a dark, sticky hole.

Too weary to move, he just let out a groan . . .
then got a strange feeling he wasn't alone!

Out of the gloom came mysterious shapes—
a dried-up banana and two moldy grapes.
"Oh dear," said the pea. "What happened to you?"

"We were naughty," they said.
"We all ran away too.

We don't recommend it," they whimpered quite sadly.
"You'll get old and wrinkled and start to smell badly."

"I've changed my mind," said the runaway pea.
"I'll get back on that plate where I really should be."

"You won't," said the grapes,
"'cause you've been on the floor.
Runaway pea, you're not
loved anymore."

The little pea trembled. He knew it was true.
There was nowhere to go for him, nothing to do.

Helpless and hopeless and feeling forlorn,
his tired eyes closed and he gave a big yawn.

But a magic thing happened while he was asleep . . .

. . . he woke up beside
the recycling heap.

The soil was soft and the weather was sunny,
and soon the pea started to feel a bit funny.

Under the ground he was sprouting some roots,
and out of his top he was shooting out shoots!

The shoots all had pods, and inside every one
was a party of new peas, all bursting with fun!

So if you should ever hear
POP, PING, or SPLAT,

or a **SPLOSH** in the sink,
or a **YOW** from the cat,

or a RAPPERTY TAP in the cupboard, then please . . .

DON'T PANIC,

it's only those runaway peas!

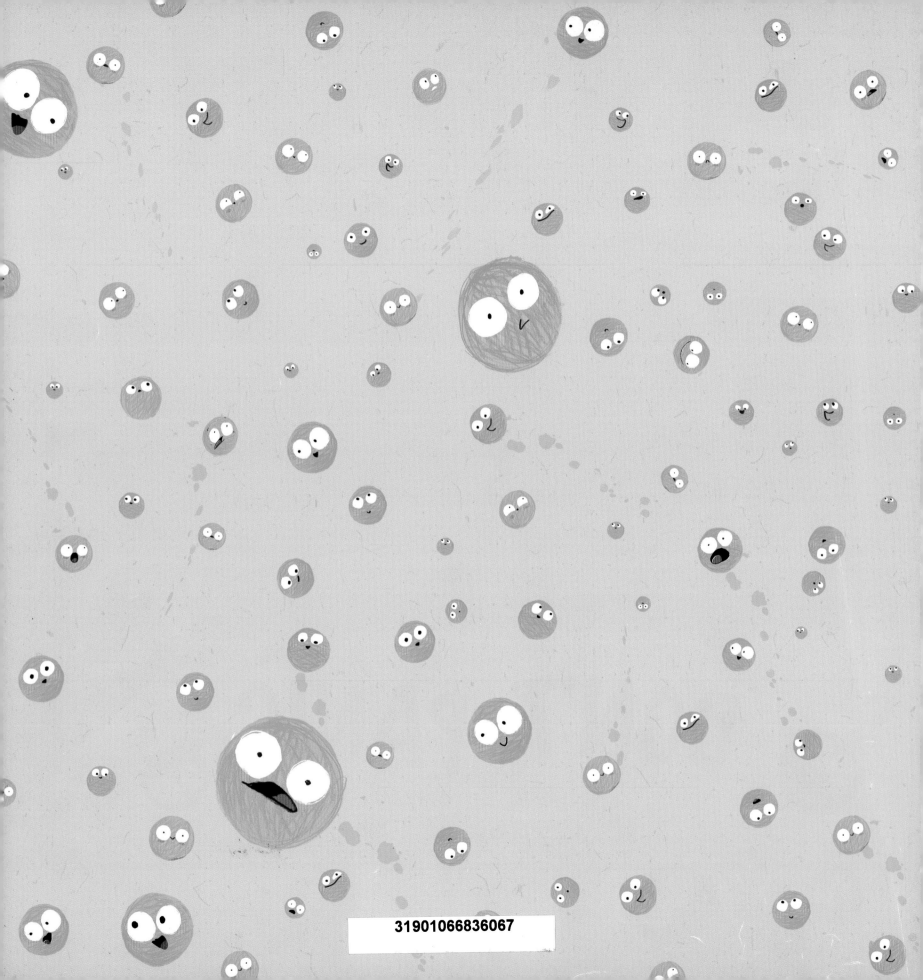